# THE HERRING MAN

Born in Saundersfoot, Cyril James Morris joined the Royal Navy as an apprentice at age sixteen. He served twenty-two years as a marine and aeronautical engineer, followed by training as a helicopter anti-submarine pilot and eventually as a helicopter maintenance test pilot. After his retirement he became a lobster fisherman in Saundersfoot for a couple of years and then took up a position in the U.S.A. as an aerostat flight director. He returned to Saundersfoot in 2014 to pursue his writing.

# THE HERRING MAN

## Cyril James Morris

PARTHIAN

Parthian, Cardigan SA43 1ED
www.parthianbooks.com
© Cyril James Morris 2022
Print ISBN: 978-1-913640-61-3
Ebook ISBN: 978-1-913640-89-7
Cover Design: Syncopated Pandemonium
Typeset by Elaine Sharples
Printed by 4edge Limited
Published with the financial support of the Books Council of Wales
British Library Cataloguing in Publication Data
A cataloguing record for this book is available from the British Library.

'It is an ancient Mariner,
And he stoppeth one of three…'

This story is dedicated to:
'They that go down to the sea in *small* ships'

My gratitude to Carly Holmes, the editor of this book, for her professionalism and guidance in arranging the matters that authors overlook or take for granted

# THE
# OLD MAN

........................

There is a story never told
That tears away my heart and soul,
May I behold that beauteous day
When all my fears are cast away
And I give back all that was lost
Back to the sea that ever tossed
Them on this sacred shore.

# CHAPTER 1

......................

It never ceased to amaze him how in the summertime the early rising sun over Carmarthen Bay streamed through the small window and accurately framed the shadow of two of the four window frames surrounding the glass panes on to the far wall, highlighting his ancestors. On the right was his father. A black and white image, shoulders bent over the gunnels of a boat, spoke-shave in hand, smoothing the fine ash topside. He had been a boat-builder and the one in his picture, a substantial, open-topped clinker rowing boat, was the last one he built. Determined to finish it before he passed on. The boat was still there, completed with a fine pair of oars resting in galvanised rowlocks, but now unused, paint fading, resting in the garden outside that overlooked the beach. The bow of the boat attached by a clip to a rusty steel cable leading to an even rustier hand-winch.

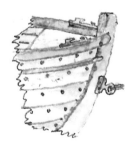

To the left of his father's picture was a faded sepia photograph of his grandfather, just as he remembered him in his old fishing smock and sailor's cap. Weathered, people would probably say, and they would be right, but he remembered the crinkly eyes and, best of all, the stories he told him when he was a boy as he taught him how to mend his nets with one of the two ivory needles that still hung either side of a brass key on the bottom of the picture frame. Those were the good days.

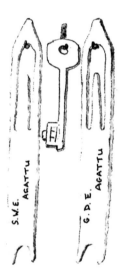

Perhaps it was now his turn. He'd thought about it for a long time, but the pain never went away. He lived on his own since his wife died. No son or daughter to pass them on to, but the stories should not die. They were part of a family's heritage. They ought to be remembered by someone, somewhere, somehow. No-one else could do it, he was the only one left and he wasn't sure how many more years he had before the stories would be lost forever.

He shifted to make himself more comfortable in his grandfather's kitchen chair alongside the oak table next to the old range. To the right of the fire was a box full of driftwood picked up from the beach. On the side of the box was a single word '**CRAN**,' painted in blue; Grandfather's favourite colour, the ever-changing colour of the sky and sea. His gaze shifted to the badly painted sign that was propped up against the wall under the window. At the beginning of the summer he had painted it. Every day since then he had looked at it, undecided if he had the courage. He should, he knew that. He should have put it up outside in the garden weeks ago, but he hadn't, had he? Taking a final slurp of lukewarm tea he slid the mug back onto the table, got up, stretched, collected his net-needle, picked up the sign and carried it into the garden. It was a first step. The easy bit, but could he follow through?

# CHAPTER 2

........................

The teenage boy with the tousled black hair and tatty beige T-shirt was there again at the bottom of the shallow, sloping, concrete slipway that led from the back garden to the beach. He remembered seeing him yesterday and the day before in the same place, staring. Or rather a part of him, the upper torso, only the head and shoulders, the boat outside concealing the rest of his body. He'd hung around for a while before wandering off towards the harbour. Today he seemed in no hurry to move on. What did he want? What was he looking at so intently? Maybe he should ask him, but the doubts crept in again. He knew most of the boys in the village but only by sight. He never talked to them. He hadn't spoken to anyone since that tragic night. Not to his father or his wife. Not anyone. It was weeks back then, how many he could not remember, before he could even do anything. In the end his father had made him get on with mending the damaged nets. Now they were locked in the shed, half hidden behind a stack of boxes, since he couldn't bear to fish anymore.

Shed was the wrong word. It was more like an Aladdin's cave. It was his father's workshop where he kept the tools and equipment to build boats. That was his passion and how he made his living. Most of the boats in the harbour were constructed by him. His tools were a cacophony of saws of every ilk, chisels, spokeshaves, clamps and more basic tools like hammers, mallets and screwdrivers. Hand tools were his trade and that was all he needed to build a boat. Hanging from the beams were old port and starboard oil lamps picked up from junk shops and jumble sales. There were brass fairleads for mooring ropes and all sorts of bow-shackles in different sizes. He carved all the floats for the nets from local wood. Cork was a rarity picked up from the beach. Lead weights were moulded for the bottom of the nets from lead piping melted down on an old primus stove. Surprisingly, amongst the junk, was his wife's old typewriter from her secretarial days. He never threw anything away.

He couldn't remember when he'd last opened the shed to put a full box of pebbles or a new net inside. There were six boxes already there, one on top of the other. It had taken a long time to fill them. The seventh and last one was outside not yet filled. It wasn't just a question of picking up any old pebble as he walked along the beach. It had to be a certain size, colour and shape. It took ages to fill a box, months, some of them years. Before he went out looking, he would remove the least desirably shaped pebble from the box in the hope that he could replace it with a better one.

Grandfather had a thing about the number seven. He said it was the most important number in not only this world but also in the stars. He was always talking about it: the Seven Wonders of the World, the Seven Great Continents, Africa, Antarctica, Asia, Australia, Europe, North America and South America. Then of course the Seven Pillars of Wisdom as in the Bible and the Seven Sisters in the sky and many more. His favourite was the seven colours of the rainbow. A message from the skies. He always went fishing if he saw a rainbow. Perhaps that's why he decided to sail the Seven Seas to find out about these things and that's where all his stories came from. He always used seven nets knotted together with a bowline when he was fishing. Each net was seventy feet long, a total length of four hundred and ninety feet of net, and he always set his nets in seven fathoms of water, at a depth of forty-two feet where the herrings spawned.

To please the memory of his grandfather he made new nets all the time, just like *he* had made, in groups of seven that he knew he would never use, but it helped to pass the time. They were stored in the shed. That was why as he worked the sheet-bend knots with his net-needle he had come to the conclusion that he had to pass on the stories. He was thinking all this while the boy was watching him.

He must be a visitor down with his family for the school holidays. Should he say something to him, any-thing? But it was as if he had forgotten how to talk.

The boy broke the awkward silence.

'Is that your boat, mister?'

He tried to respond but he couldn't speak the words. Instead he just nodded, dropped the sign and hurried back inside. Through the window he watched the boy scratching his head and looking back, puzzled, as he retreated to the beach.

He should have said something to the boy, but it was so hard. He felt ashamed. Next time he would try harder, if there was a next time. Perhaps the boy wouldn't come back. He should have put up the sign. It was lying upside down in the garden. He would rescue it...

There, it was now safe inside propped again under the window wall. He wiped off the smear of mud, sat back and looked at it. He read the words on the sign in his mind, painted in shaky blue letters on a pale background. The blue was the same colour as the blue on the boat outside before it faded and on the **CRAN** box by the fire. It was the paint left over from when his father was alive. He remembered his father cleaning brushes, and his cracked hands, the smell of turpentine. He pictured the words and read them again to himself.

Could he say it aloud? Maybe. There was no one around to listen just now but there would have to be if he put the sign outside. He shifted his gaze to his grandfather's photograph. He seemed to be willing him on. Could he, like his grandfather, tell the stories? He knew them off by heart and had practised them in his mind in order to be able to pass them on.

'Sss SssT SssTORY TELLER.' He thought his grandfather smiled. Inside his mind he heard him.

*Tell them from the beginning.*

And so he started, found his voice and softly told the room the very first tale he'd heard from his grandfather. The one about crossing one of the Seven Seas, the North Atlantic, through that magical place the Sargasso Sea where strange creatures never seen anywhere before crawled on floating seaweed. He said their black eyes blinked as they waved their antennae and claws at him as he sat at the tiller and slowly sailed past great rafts of coloured seaweeds in reds, yellows, greens, blues, pinks and browns. Like a miniature forest in autumn was how he'd described it. He'd had that way of saying things that conjured up the images so that they were easily remembered. Could *he* do that?

This was not so very different from telling the stories inside his head. Though here inside the room there was no-one watching him, listening. Faces. People. He remembered hearing somewhere that there was an ancient inn, a meeting place in the Brecon Beacons where old men drank beer and swapped stories about Merlin and Geraldus Cambrensis that had somehow been recorded in the granite walls of the building. A group of magical modern Merlins using an electronic listening device found them. This could be his way out. To tell his stories to the cottage so that in the future someone would find them. He would not have to face anyone then other than his grandfather. He looked across but was dismayed to see that Grandfather was shaking his head. He knew now that he was still not ready, and the summer was coming to an end. The visitors would no longer be around. It was a relief. There would always be next year. His grandfather looked sad and below the frame there was a net-needle missing. He must have dropped it when the boy startled him. He would go and look.

He couldn't find it. It wasn't there. He searched high and low in the grass, under the boat, by the shed, around the net where he had been intending to work. It could have bounced anywhere. He had to find it. His grandfather carved it for him from a walrus tusk that he was given in Alaska, but that was another tale for the telling. He had also engraved it with his own initials G.D.E., just like his grandfather's needle. In the end as the sun went down behind the cottage and the light faded, he gave up. He would resume the search in the morning.

# CHAPTER 3

........................

Next day he could just see through the rain-spattered window that the beach was deserted. A September westerly gale carried the horizontal rain off the Atlantic, buffeting the cottage. He debated whether to go out but the storm wasn't what bothered him. He might bump into the boy and that would be difficult. On his mind was the lost net-needle. It had to be somewhere in the garden. He must find it. Despite the storm he would take another look, followed by a walk on the beach. The boy might not be around in this weather. Donning his oilskins and sou'wester he went outside. It had to be there somewhere, but where? He still couldn't find it. Giving up for the time being he selected a pebble from the half empty, or was it half full, box, pocketed it and made his way down the slipway to the beach.

It had been blowing all night and the surf had tossed new pebbles on to the shore and scoured the sand, revealing newly exposed shingle. Watery eyes down, carefully scrutinising the stones, he began a new search. The pebbles wet from the rain disguised the colour so it would be difficult, but he always first looked for the size and shape. The colour and the holes drilled by the most delicate bivalve, the piddock, the shell that even glows in the dark, would help to determine if it was a keeper. How this fragile creature was able to drill into solid stone he never knew. Grandfather would have known but when he was alive it wasn't relevant as he never collected pebbles then.

After a fruitless hour or more on the beach he returned to the cottage a little dejected but not surprised that he hadn't picked up a replacement pebble. On the positive side he'd had the beach to himself and hadn't had to interact with anyone, especially the boy. Placing the original pebble carefully back into the box and aligning it with the others he turned to re-enter the cottage. There it was, his net-needle, on the stool where he usually worked on the nets. It hadn't been there earlier, he was certain. In that instant he knew. It had to be the boy from yesterday. No-one else had seen him there. He would have to thank him. He would have to ask him that first. That would be very difficult, involving a lot of words. Could he do it? He didn't know.

He experienced an unusual feeling as he picked the net-needle up. Something like a small electric shock but more a tingling through his hand and fingers. He put it back down on the stool and the sensation went away. He picked it up again and an image of the boy flashed through his mind. Inside the cottage once more with the net-needle hanging back in its proper place he thought of the boy. He knew now that he would have to speak to him and in a strange way a calmness come over him. It was almost as if he was looking forward to it, but it was too easy to think like that. When it came to talking, it was a different matter. He would watch for him in the days ahead.

# CHAPTER 4

........................

Five days of looking out of the window had slipped by with no sign of the boy. He was sure, now that the holidays were over, that he had returned with his parents to where they lived. In a way he was relieved but also disappointed. He thought that maybe he could even have spoken to him about the net-needle and showed him how to use it. Well, the opportunity was lost. It would have to be next year, if he was lucky.

Grandfather always said that knowledge and luck went together. That you based your decisions on facts, but you needed a little luck on your side to enable them to be fulfilled. After he'd passed out of the Sargasso Sea, he had headed northward to a place he had heard of known as 'The Little Grey Lady of the Sea'. An island off the Northeast coast of America. He should tell the boy the story when he came next year. If he came next year.

Saturday morning. He hadn't done any net-making all week as he had been hoping to see the boy. It was time to get back outside into his usual routine.

'Can I look at your boat, mister?'

Grandfather was right. Sometimes you needed a little luck. The boy was there. Where had he come from? He hadn't been there when he'd looked out of the window.

He nodded and waved his hand toward the boat and the boy grinned and went to look.

'The brightwork needs cleaning. I can do it for you, if you like? Have you got any Brasso?'

He knew that the boy was right. He hadn't had the heart to work on the boat for a long time. It needed some attention. There was probably some Brasso in the shed, but he didn't want the boy searching around in there on his own. However, he could hardly refuse such a simple request. He indicated to the boy to wait by the shed as he went inside the cottage for the brass key.

The key turned easily in the well-oiled lock, and the boy followed him into the dimly-lit shed. Like silken-threaded lace the cobwebs clung to the windows, competing with the herring nets dangling from the rafters to catch unwary insects instead of fish. There on a shelf was a can, the word Brasso struggling to be read under the dust. He gave it to the boy, who was gazing curiously around, together with some rags, and eased him out of the door. Locking it behind him as there were too many painful secrets hidden inside amongst the ageing chandlery.

The boy worked diligently polishing the fairleads, the brass around the small binnacle compass on the bow platform and the mooring cleats, whistling to himself. The man stole glances at him from time to time, wondering if he might say something else.

'What's that fish?' asked the boy, pointing to the painting of a silver fish on the boat, near the bow underneath the name *Winston*.

He had to reply, there was no way he could wave his hands again.

'H hh herring.' The sounds stumbled out as if he heard them from somewhere in the distant past.

'D'you catch them here?'
He nodded.
'How?' persisted the boy.

He waved again. 'N nn nets,' and pointed to the one he was working on.

The boy came over and gingerly touched the fine twine of the net hanging from a rope slung between the top of the shed and a pole at the bottom of the garden.

'Show me?'

And that was how the stilted conversation began and slowly gathered pace.

He showed him how to make the knot to weave the mesh.

'See.'

The boy nodded. 'Can I try?'

'Wait.' And he went inside to fetch his grandfather's net-needle for the boy to try his hand.

'Not like that. Like this.'

He soon caught on to the technique and together in silence they worked in unison. It was like a dream. Like the days when he'd worked with his grandfather doing the same thing. Except that Grandfather had always hummed or sang softly as he worked or fished. Singing was important for the soul, he'd said, and at one time it had saved his life. That was another story that he would tell the boy, but not yet.

'What do these letters and the word Agattu on the needle stand for? asked the boy.

'They're my grandfather's initials and Agattu is an island where he got the ivory for the net needles.' He couldn't quite believe how easily the words came out.

'What was his name?'

'Samuel Winston Evans. His older friends called him Sam the Herring Man.'

'Why did they call him that?'

'Because he liked to catch herrings.'

'I never had a grandfather.'

'You must have. Everybody has or had a grandfather.'

'I never had a father.'

He stared at the boy, a sudden lump in his throat preventing him uttering any new words.

'It's always been just me and my mum. We've just moved here.'

So that was why he was still around, and he hadn't seen him all week. He was in school here.

'What's it like having a grandfather?'

The boy was full of questions.

'He told me about his adventures and taught me a lot.' He wanted to say *I loved him,* but again the words wouldn't come.

'What did he do?'

More questions. 'He was a fisherman but before that he was a sailor and he sailed around the world.' The stories and images leapt into his mind.

'That's amazing. I'd like to be a fisherman. Was that his boat?'

He shook his head and knew that the conversation couldn't go any further, he would have to change it quickly.

'Would you like to see his picture? Come with me and bring the net-needle.'

The boy followed him into the cottage.

'There,' he said with a flourish as he hung both net-needles back underneath the photo either side of the brass key. 'That's my grandfather.'

'He looks very old there. When did he stop fishing?'

'Never. He had his nets in the water the day before he died.'

The boy looked back at him in amazement.

'And that's my father, he built the boat that is outside.' As the boy looked at the second image, the old man took the opportunity to turn the sign towards the wall.

'Why isn't the boat in the harbour like the other fishing boats?'

'Grandfather always said "If I answer all your questions, you'll be as wise as me." You'll have to go now. I have things to do. If you are interested and can come next weekend, I might tell you a bit more about Grandfather,' and without waiting for an answer, and with some relief, he shuffled the boy out.

Too many questions that he knew could not be easily answered. Yet he liked the boy.

# CHAPTER 5

........................

The following weekend when the boy came and before the myriad of questions bombarded him, he kept his promise, sat him down and told him about Grandfather's first trip across the Atlantic, through the Sargasso Sea and north-west towards an island off the east coast of America. Grandfather always said if you make a promise you must keep it.

He told the boy that Grandfather navigated by the pole star, threading his way through the myriad islands of the Bahamas by night and day, sailing over weed-covered, hidden, sunken galleons loaded with treasure

looted from the Spanish Main now guarded by monstrous moray eels. He marvelled at the flying fish not much larger than swallows as they skittered over the water away from the hull of his sloop the *Clupea Man*.

With sketchbook in hand and the tiller lashed, each day he recorded what he saw. The hurricane season had come and gone, the sea like a millpond, the sky hazy with patches of sea fog drifting over the surface of the water. It engulfed his small craft with its flat sails and he waited anxiously for the next puff of wind to carry him into the Gulf Stream that would move him steadily northwards towards his landfall. His fishing line trailed the boat, hoping to catch a Spanish or King Mackerel for tea. Further up the coast under the influence of the Gulf Stream and a light wind from the south the advection fog thickened. Grandfather said that advection fog was caused by warm, moist air passing over a cold surface, be it either land or water. It is why sailors gave the island he was looking for its local name, 'The Little Grey Lady of the Sea', because it was often shrouded in mist and difficult to find.

Grandfather was a remarkable sailor. He knew land was nearby from the smell of steaming blubber and whale oil permeating the air, and the increasing number of birds on the water, fearful of flying blind in the fog. He made his ghostly landfall on Nantucket Island, appearing out of the mist in his small boat like some extinct sea creature, and was immediately welcomed in the town by the Algonquin whalers and residents who fed him salt cod fattened by the vast shoals of Atlantic herring and caught over the Newfoundland Banks.

The old man paused, drew a breath, sat back and looked at the boy. He could not quite believe what he had done; told a real person the first of many stories.

# CHAPTER 6

........................

The following Saturday the boy was there again leaning against the hull of the fishing boat. He went out to meet him.

'Look, the paint's peeling off the boat, it needs re-painting,' he said pointing. 'I can do it if you like?'

He was right. It did need painting. It was remiss of him as he should have done it some time ago, but he always had other things on his mind. There was paint in the shed, he knew that, but it meant allowing the boy in there again. That worried him. Then he remembered what Grandfather had said, that a man was worthy of his hire. He should give the boy a chance and pay him for the job, but not today. There were things that he had to do before he allowed the boy into the shed again, now he knew that the boy was curious about almost everything and was fascinated by the contents of the shed.

Somewhat reluctantly he agreed. 'But not today. If you can come tomorrow, I will find what you need for the job. Sandpaper, scrapers, brushes, paint, stirrers, white spirit and anything else I can think of.'

'I can help you do that.'

'No. I'm busy today. You should come tomorrow, or next week, and I will pay you.'

'I don't need any pay. I like to help. Perhaps you would tell me another story instead?'

'Tomorrow then. It looks like rain today. You can't paint in the rain. Tomorrow then.'

'What about the nets. I could do some of that?'

He was persistent.

'No! Go now and come back tomorrow if you like. I have things to do.' He turned and almost marched back into the cottage. After waiting a little while he peeked out of the window and was relieved to see that the boy was no longer there. It had been awkward. He didn't like doing it, but it had to be, and he knew that it wasn't going to rain.

Later that day when he was sure that the boy was no longer nearby, he took the key and ventured outside meaning to sort out the difficulties in the shed before gathering together the painting materials. As was his habit, before he went to the shed, he checked the box of pebbles by the wall and was amazed to find a perfect new pebble lying correctly alongside the others. Only the boy could have done it, but why, and how had he known? Disturbing memories overcame him as his eyes welled up. He wiped away a tear before seeking refuge back inside his cottage.

Three weekends later the boy finished painting the boat. There had been much ancillary work prior to the actual painting job, like initial washing, sanding, re-caulking of some of the clinker planking that had shrunk as it dried out due to the boat being open to all weathers. With guidance from the old man he had stuck to his task despite the difficulties, and now he stood back admiring his handiwork.

'What do you think?' he said to the old man.

'Very good,' he replied, not wanting to be too enthusiastic, sensing where this might be leading.

'Can we put it in the harbour now and you can teach me how to fish?'

'There's a lot more to do before that can happen but I promised to tell you another story about Grandfather's adventures after you'd painted the boat. Now is the time,' he said, changing the subject. 'Come inside and I will tell you what happened after Nantucket. You remember that's where we left off previously.'

# CHAPTER 7

..........................

After a week or two in Nantucket resting, re-provisioning and getting to know the whalers, Grandfather departed. He followed them, sailing onwards toward two more of the Seven Seas, the first one the South Atlantic, replicating their voyages to their traditional whaling grounds and then on into the Pacific Ocean. In his small boat he could not keep up with their faster, heavier ships with huge fore and aft dirt-stained sails billowing and bellowing

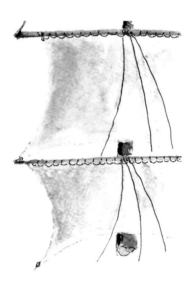

to each gust of wind like massive thunderclouds and he was often overtaken by others following the same route in a race to be first to the place where they knew that their livelihoods depended.

En route he traced the coastline of South America and stood well out to sea to avoid pirates nearer the shore bent on capturing any unwary boat foolish enough to stray too close. Even miles from the coast the mighty Amazon river's muddy waters were still evident, sluicing the sea with sediment and nutrients washed from the great rainforests of Brazil. Grandfather explained to me at one time about buoyancy, that fresh water was lighter than the salty sea and it floated on the surface.

Further south Grandfather said he was buffeted by fierce storms but that he managed to shelter in the Magellan Straits near the tip of South America, Tierra del Fuego. One night whilst sheltering there he dreamed of Magellan the Portuguese sailor who discovered the passage through the straits. In the dream he was told to follow the albatross that would lead him to the "peaceful sea" as Magellan called it. Sure enough, the next morning the huge bird flew over him and he followed it as instructed through the straits, collecting a favourable breeze on his way, into the Pacific Ocean.

Grandfather liked poetry and he had with him Samuel Taylor Coleridge's book of poems. It reminded the old man of the 'Rime of the Ancient Mariner' that his grand-father read to him when he was a boy.

'What's that all about and what kind of bird is an albatross? I've never heard of it.'

The old man paused. 'Do you like to read?' he asked the boy.

'Not much,' he replied.

'Pity,' said the old man. 'I still have his book here somewhere. I'll give it to you if I can find it. You should read it and you will find the answers to all your questions.'

'Maybe. What happened next?'

But the old man had run out of talk for stories for the time being. He wanted to ask the boy about the new pebble that he must have placed in the box, and to tell him to remove one not as good, but he wasn't sure how to go about it. He would be bound to ask why he, the old man, was collecting special pebbles, and he couldn't and wouldn't want to explain. Better that he kept his counsel and said nothing.

# THE BOY

........................

Oars dipping softly through time and space
As words in the current of life gather pace.
A boy, now a man with a *"father"* again
Sets him free from a life, stricken with pain.

# CHAPTER 8

..........................

It's been more than a year now since I left school and so much has happened. I am gradually beginning to understand. My friend the old man eventually told me the rest of Grandfather's story, and that's what I have come to know him as, as well as: Grandfather. The old man the father I'd never had. I heard about his trip up through the Pacific to the Alaskan islands, in particular to one of the very small islands in the Aleut chain, Agattu Island. It is one of those almost unbelievable stories, that I'm sure was true, that Grandfather passed on to him, but more of that later.

I had asked Father if there was any silver paint in the shed as I wanted to re-paint the image of the herring on either side of the bow of the boat. He wouldn't let me into the shed again to help him find it and I was beginning to sense that therein was some secret that he couldn't share. On the day that I was due to re-paint the herrings, that's when I found him. He was in the kitchen slumped over the oak table, a mug spilled and cold tea dripping on to the floor. By the wall under the window was a sign that had always been turned towards the wall so I couldn't read it but now it had been turned around. On it was painted in wobbly letters:

In front of him, skewed to one side, was the old Olivetti typewriter that I remembered seeing in the shed the first and only time he allowed me in there. Two books, one on top of the other, were protected by his right hand. I didn't know what to do, he was obviously

dead. I'd never seen a dead person before. The paper caught my eye, the typewriter reluctant to release it. It read: *Exchange the pebbles. Here is the poetry book I promised you and I found Grandfather's old log.* Then finally in capital letters: *TELL THEM THE STORIES.* But how could I, I knew hardly any of them yet?

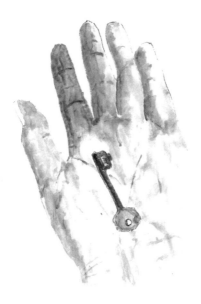

The brass key was in his other hand, palm up as if he was offering it to someone. I assumed it was for me, so I took the key, the books and the note from the typewriter and went home before the enormity of it dawned on me. Sadly, and with a sense of loss, I told my mother and she called the authorities...

The police ordered me to come back to the cottage. The silver paint pot was still outside with a fine brush resting on top. Anxiously I went in. The old man was gone. He had vanished as if he had never been there. A policeman sat at the table on Father's usual chair staring at the typewriter. He looked at me and indicated for me to sit. Watching me carefully he wanted to know if there had been a note in the typewriter or on the table. I shook my head. I think that he thought that the old man had committed suicide. I knew that he hadn't. There had been times when there seemed to be a sadness about him that made him a little crotchety, especially when I wanted to go into the shed. I'd just thought that was his nature. Now I suspected that he might have been ill and like many other things he hid it.

I was asked about my relationship with the old man and I said we were just friends and that I'd helped him with the boat and a few other things. I was told that there would have to be an autopsy to determine the cause of death and that I should stay away from the cottage. I didn't like that and explained about the paint outside. He said I could do that little job, but the cottage would be locked up until matters were settled. Then he let me go.

Time went by slowly. I wanted to buy the boat and become a fisherman but we, my mother and I, had little spare money for that sort of thing. I got a job of sorts, but it didn't pay much. On the first weekend I painted the herrings on the boat as I'd promised, taking care to highlight all the tiny scales, remembering that Grandfather had said *If you made a promise, you must keep it.* I thought about putting the paint back into the shed as I had the key but decided it would be a bad idea, so I just put the paint pot and brush under the boat. I kept thinking about the message that Father had left, especially the part that read, *Exchange the pebbles.* The box was still there by the white wall with its pebbles neatly lined up in rows, and I looked at it each time I went to the beach. One day I picked up a likely looking pebble and took it to the box. As I went to lay it alongside the others it didn't quite match up. Then it dawned on me, *Exchange the pebbles* meant that only the best would be suitable no matter how long it took to find them. I continued with the search each time I went to the beach. My father, as I realised I now regarded him as, would have liked that I knew.

Weeks later an official looking letter arrived for me from a firm of solicitors in a nearby town requesting me to call on them at my convenience as they had some information for me about a Mr. Gwyn Dorian Evans. They gave the address of the cottage on the beach. Gwyn Dorian Evans; I had never heard his name, but it had to be Father. I recognised the initials G.D.E. carved into his net-needle. He had bequeathed everything to me in his will: the house, boat, and shed plus all the contents. The autopsy had been performed and nothing unusual was found so now it was up to my mother and I to arrange his funeral. His will also said that he was to be cremated and his ashes to be scattered in Carmarthen Bay.

It was a sad time. My mother and I and two older local fishermen were the only ones at the funeral. They seemed to know something of Father's past but were unwilling to talk about him. One of them offered to take me out in his boat to scatter the ashes. I respectfully declined. It was something that I wanted to do by myself when the time was right. The urn sat on the mantelpiece over the hearth awaiting my readiness to perform his final wish and say my last goodbyes. The sign with the blue lettering about becoming a **STORY TELLER** remained by the window wall but the summer was nearly over. It would have to wait until the following year if at all. In the meantime, there was Grandfather's log and book of poems to be studied and more importantly the real story that Father had never shared.

LOG BOOK
CLUPEA MAN
Samuel Winston
Evans

# CHAPTER 9

·························

I started with the book of poems. I'd never been a reader and my command of English was quite poor, but I remembered what Father had said when he was telling me about Grandfather's passage through the Magellan Straits. He was disappointed when I told him that I didn't read much if at all and when I questioned him about a bird that I'd never heard of, the albatross, he told me to read the poem and my questions would be answered. Was there more to that reply than I'd understood at the time, I wondered? He said that the albatross was a lucky bird, and it must have been because it led Grandfather through the Magellan Straits into the open water of the Pacific, but the poem told the opposite because the Ancient Mariner shot the albatross that led to his incredible bad luck. It took me a long time to read the poem as it had more than a hundred verses and within those verses were many words that I never understood. I found an old dictionary in the cottage and each time I came across an unknown word I looked up its meaning.

Like I said earlier, Father told me that Grandfather sailed to Alaska and on the way encountered a pod of whales feeding on vast shoals of Pacific herring. Their mouths like Fingal's Cave, he said, swallowing hundreds, nay thousands of fish with each gape. He enlightened me about Fingal's Cave sometime later, but I sensed the vastness of it at the time. Grandfather told him that God had packed the sea with herrings to feed all creatures including man. The whalers came as he was watching and bloodied the blue ocean with their endeavours. Grandfather couldn't bear to watch and sailed on northwards to the Aleutian Islands.

I read on and, for my own education, found paper in an old cupboard and started to use the typewriter. I typed every word that I didn't know together with its meaning. The words on each page in the dictionary were to me an understanding of the importance of language, and the whole book of words was like the ocean filled to overflowing with fish. My shallow typing of words gradually became sentences and the sentences paragraphs of words complementing one another like shoals of swimming fish. It captured my imagination and I turned my attention to Grandfather's log thinking all the time of Father's last words on the paper: *TELL THEM THE STORIES*.

# CHAPTER 10

..........................

I found myself in somewhat of a dilemma, too many important tasks and I was unsure which one to tackle first. Father's ashes seemed to be the most pressing but to achieve that I had to get the boat into the water, and I had never rowed a boat before in my life. I would need to practise. However, I was comfortable for the time being knowing that Father was still there in the cottage with me. The rusty hand-winch had seized up and when I tried to turn the handle to ease the tension on the cable attached to the boat in order to release the spring clip, it would not budge. That meant a visit to the shed for tools and grease and an opportunity for the first time to explore inside on my own. I collected the brass key from its hook under Grandfather's photo where I had replaced it when I moved to the cottage. Mother wouldn't come as she had a job that paid enough for her to rent her own small flat and she was happy there. I had been putting off a visit to the shed. Each time I picked up the key it seemed to me, when looking at the urn, that Father was uncomfortable with my proposed expedition. At such times I felt that it should wait until after I had scattered his ashes in the sea, but I couldn't do that until I got the boat into the water. In the end I came to the conclusion that the answer was to get what I needed for the winch without exploring any further. I think that Father approved as I felt no more discomfort when I looked at his urn.

It only took me a few days to de-rust, oil and grease the winch back into action but I had to wait another week for the spring tides that lapped the slipway before I could launch. That week after three outings I became reasonably proficient at launching, rowing, handling and recovering the boat. I discovered that there cannot be anything as magical as rowing a boat on a silent moonlit night. The sparkling phosphorescence as the oar dips into the water, the creak of the leather padding between the oar and rowlock, and the splash of a nearby fish startled by this silent, surface intrusion. I knew that I was now ready to carry out Father's last wishes.

The next set of evening high spring tides were the obvious time to carry out those wishes and scatter his ashes in the bay. I rowed out as the sun set, but where to? Father had not said exactly where. I thought about what the solicitor said about it in the will and something struck me as odd. I must admit that I am slow in grasping the meaning of things but the more I thought of it the clearer it became. I returned to the shore and replaced the urn on the mantelpiece. I had never read the will that had been eventually forwarded to me. There was a clue of sorts there I suspected, something to do with what the solicitor had said. I spread the pages of the document out on the table and looked for the part about Father's last wishes. There it was in black and white "...scatter his ashes in Carmarthen Bay." Not "...scatter MY ashes in Carmarthen Bay," but "...scatter HIS ashes in Carmarthen Bay." Whose ashes was Father referring to, if not his own?

# CHAPTER 11

..........................

I continued to work through Grandfather's log while I tried to figure out what had gone on in Father's past. It took me seven months to go through the records and translate his journeys, recorded in sketches and voluminous notes into my own words. One month for each story of the Seven Seas he traversed. It became my way of ensuring that Father's past family and their stories would not be forgotten. Over the months, although I often rowed out into Carmarthen Bay, the urge to become a fisherman gradually waned. I became more comfortable in front of the Olivetti. When summer came around once more, I repainted the letters on the sign that Father had made to make them clearer and displayed it outside in the garden. I began by relating some of Grandfather's stories to the few people who stopped by and cared to listen, but my writings, if they could be called a book, would be my way of passing on the tales to a wider audience.

One of my favourite stories of Grandfather's adventures took place when he was in Alaska. Time after time in his log he would bring up surprising things that had occurred wherever he was in his oceanic location. He said it was always the unexpected way of things. On Agattu Island he saved the life of an Aleutian boy. Those are my words. Grandfather told it differently.

He wrote in his log that he was beachcombing on Agattu Island when he came across an Aleut boy straddling a dead walrus; he had just finished cutting out the ivory tusks of the beast. Grandfather estimated that he was some five to ten yards from the boy who stood up smiling and waving his prize. What the boy could not see approaching from behind him was a huge polar bear, its jaws dripping wet with fresh, red blood and staining its sleek white fur, intent it appeared to savage any intrusion to his prey. The boy sensed Grandfather's stare and turned towards the threat. Frightened, he began to run. Grandfather grabbed his arm and pushed him behind his back and told him not to run as it would incense the animal into attack. Instead, Grandfather began to sing. He knew that all creatures responded to music. He sang that wonderful Welsh lullaby 'Myfanwy' in his best chapel baritone as he backed the boy and himself slowly away. The polar bear paused in its approach, listening, and with a wary eye and a grunt of satisfaction laid itself over the carcass.

Grandfather added in his log how unusual an experience it was to see a walrus, although they are common in Alaska at certain times of the year, and also a polar bear, carried this far south probably on an ice floe. The boy insisted that Grandfather have one of the tusks and would not take no for an answer. That is the tusk from which grandfather carved the net needles.

The next full moon the boy took Grandfather night-fishing to a deep tidal inlet, in his small open boat. They caught the fabled silver tube. Grandfather wrote that he had heard of the silver tube from other herring fishers but had never experienced it himself. There were so many fish, Pacific herrings, that as the boy hauled the net the fish were so tightly packed it appeared like a silver tube rising from the dark depths surrounded by a myriad of silver scales drifting from the moonlit sky like Alaskan snowflakes.

Of all the times that I rowed into the bay, for me the best were in the evening or on those moonlit nights. It reminded me of Grandfather's silver tube, and I wondered if there were enough herrings in our bay for a catch like that to be possible. Father had told me that Grandfather always set his nets in seven fathoms, forty-two feet of water. How did he ascertain the depth, and how did he know when the herrings would be spawning there? As I came towards the end of Grandfather's log, I was able to think more about this and other problems. I had still not scattered Father's ashes for various reasons, most importantly the wording of the will, but also because I had to be sure where in the bay they were to be deposited. I had to get it right.

In between times I continued to seek pebbles for the box by the wall and was getting quite good at it. Soon it would be full. What I would do then I did not know.

The last time I went into the shed was when I worked on the winch, before I started to write Grandfather's stories. I remembered cleaning the silver paint off the small brush after I replaced the oil and grease. Now I re-membered noticing an odd coil of rope hanging from one of the hooks. I had meant to look at it more closely at the time, but other things occupied my mind and I forgot. When I left the shed, I hung the small paint brush on a loop of string on the outside door handle when I locked up to remind me to look at the coil of rope.

When I went to get the key from where it was hanging under Grandfather's picture it dawned on me. I have said before that I am sometimes slow at figuring things out. This was another of those times. Father had given me the key. It was held out to me as a parting gift in his hand when I found him. He wanted me to look in the shed, but in the past every time I picked up the key it seemed that he discouraged me from doing so. Why now? As I looked at the urn he still seemed to disapprove, possibly because firstly he wanted me to find something else that was not in the shed. Perhaps in the house. Wait. In his other hand he gave me the books. The log and the poetry book, surely there had to be something in one of those...

# CHAPTER 12

..........................

I went back to the log. Father's final typed note had become my bookmark positioned at the last recorded page of Grandfather's log, but there were a few more pages left before the end of the book. The next page was blank followed by a rough chart of Carmarthen Bay with what looked like navigational sketches. I recognised Caldey Island and the coastline. Three straight lines with compass directions were drawn on the chart stretching into the middle of the bay. One from Caldey lighthouse, the next from St. Mary's church spire in Tenby and the last from Monkstone Point near Saundersfoot. The three lines intersected in a place on the chart and were marked by some form of an abbreviation or code. H7F for W HT. This had to be what Father wanted me to find. H7F for W followed by HT; what did it mean? It had to be something simple. There was no grid on the rough chart so it couldn't be anything to do with latitude and longitude. Grandfather was a fisherman. This might be where he fished for herrings. H for HERRINGS and W for his name. Herrings for WINSTON. The boat outside was named *WINSTON*, his name, but it was built after Grandfather was no longer around. Father must have named it after him. Not significant though to this search.

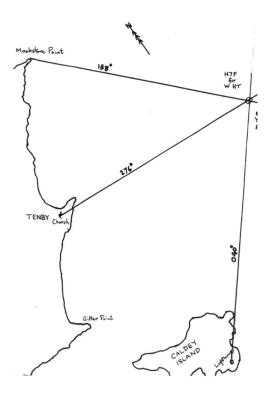

But 7F, what could that mean? I remembered Father telling me when I first met him that Grandfather set his nets in seven fathoms of water where the herrings spawned. This must be the place. I could find it with the help of the compass on the bow platform, but what about the final HT, what did that signify? I was sure now that this was where Father wanted his ashes scattered, but there it was again, I recalled the wrong word in the will: "HIS" indicating someone else's ashes. It was frustrating but having found this I felt that Father had guided me to now go ahead and search the shed.

The paint brush hanging from the doorknob reminded me of the odd coil of rope hanging inside. I took it from its hook out into the garden and uncoiled it. It was very heavy, a lead line of sorts that sailors used to plumb the depth of water beneath the ship. It had equally spaced markers along its length. I measured the distance between each marker. It was six feet, one fathom, and there were seven of them. This had to be how Grandfather determined the depth to set his nets. There was a weight at one end, some sort of iron bracket probably from a railway line. The other end, the top, was unusual. At its end there was a red marker buoy with black letters W and HT painted on it, but further down, four fathoms to be exact, there was another smaller buoy also painted with a black W and LT. I couldn't figure out what this represented. I re-coiled the rope, put it in the boat under the stern thwart and went back to the shed to continue my search.

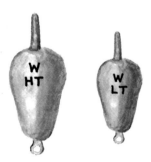

# CHAPTER 13

..........................

I had never ventured or been allowed into the dark recesses of the back of the shed. There was only a dim light from a dusty window. No electric light. It had to be a candle or a torch or even one of the ship's lanterns hanging up that illuminated it. I remembered that there was a torch on the mantelpiece next to Father's urn. It seemed appropriate. I fetched it.

In the back corner was a dingy blue canvas, a dusty boat cover draped over what looked like a tall piece of furniture. I dragged it off to reveal not furniture but a grey metal locker or cabinet. I tried the handle. It wouldn't move, it was locked with one of those flat integral locks so I couldn't break off a padlock or the hasp to gain entry. Somewhere there had to be a key. Father would know where it was. I was getting to know his mind better now. He would have left me a clue. I went back into the cottage, sat in his chair and gazed at his urn hoping that he might give me a clue. I dozed off. In my dream I saw Grandfather led by an albatross, sailing through the Magellan Straits. Then there was Father remonstrating with me for not being interested in reading Grandfather's poetry book. That was it, he had said *you should read and look through it and you will find the answers to all your questions.* Those words stuck in my head when I awoke. I had read 'The Rime of the Ancient Mariner' more than once and I knew the story of the albatross. *Look through it.* I had forgotten those words. There was something else somewhere in that book. I had to find it.

I spent days searching, reading the poetry, looking for the clue. It eluded me. *Look through it.* It was when I came to the end of the book and was about to close the back cover that I noticed it. A slight lumpiness inside the cover. I ran my finger over it. There was something hidden there. Under the cover a key. Not any old key but a flat key of the type used on a locker.

Back in the shed the key fitted. It turned readily, as did the handle, and I eased open the door.

# CHAPTER 14

...........................

I shone the torch inside and took a half step backwards. I could hardly believe what I was looking at. I bent forward to get a better look. It was a shrine. On the top shelf a cross fashioned from driftwood and bound diagonally with netting twine. On one side of the cross a peaked cap with the initial W embroidered on it, on the other a single small plimsoll and next to it an empty red cartridge case.

A gun, a rusty, twelve-bore single-barrel shotgun was propped up in the corner. On the bottom of the locker a cremation urn just like Father's but much smaller. Behind it a large white envelope. Strangest of all, hanging from a hook on the underside of the top shelf was a stocking-shaped net packed with a selection of identical pebbles beautifully painted as herrings down to the finest details of fins and scales. I counted them. There were seven. With a shaking hand I withdrew the envelope, relocked the cabinet and returned to the kitchen.

I sat there a long time staring at the envelope and thinking about the contents of the locker. The piece of net with the painted pebbles representing herrings, the same as the six full boxes of unpainted pebbles in the shed and the almost full one by the wall outside. I looked at the box full of driftwood by the fire. Painted on the side was the word **CRAN**. Seven cran of herrings. Why? I reached across and picked up the envelope. It wasn't sealed. I withdrew the contents. A few typed pages and a photograph of a young boy in tatty shorts like I used to wear, with plimsolls on his feet and a cap with a blue letter W behind the peak. I turned it over and read the name, WINSTON. It triggered a recent memory. The chart in Grandfather's log and the message H7F for W HT. I'd been wrong, the W that I'd thought was for Grandfather's name was for this boy. Herrings for WINSTON. He had to be Grandfather's great-grand-son, named after him. Father's son. I started to read the faded type. It was Father's story.

*Grandfather had always told us, Winston and I, the story of the Silver Tube that in all his years of fishing in Carmarthen Bay he had never managed to catch.*

*He said that he knew it was possible and he knew the location but that he'd never been there at that one time when the secret herrings were massing to spawn, on that one particular night probably late in November when the shoals of herring gathered to reproduce. He always kept cran boxes in his boat believing that a silver tube would fill seven of them, his lucky number. He never managed it. I was always fascinated by this and it became my sole ambition to fulfil this for Grandfather. It was to be my undoing.*

*When he was alive, Grandfather's stories were always told around the fireplace with the family seated at the kitchen table. At that time when Winston was very young, and later as he grew up and Grandfather had passed away, it was up to me to tell the stories. I knew that after I had gone Winston would pass them on to his children. I was so wrong.*

*Winston and I carried on the herring fishing tradition. Many were the nights that we hauled together and watched the seals plucking the odd fish from our nets before we got them into the boat. It was a way of sharing both with Winston and the seals. We had trouble at times from the odd dangerous shark that got entangled in our nets which was why Grandfather had advised us to carry his old shotgun in the boat to kill any shark as the boat was too small to risk landing them.*

*It was late November, the sea flat calm and a full*

*moon. I had a premonition that this might be the night and this time I was right. The net came up brimming with herrings, the silver tube at last. Winston, now quite strong for his age, hauling. Fish tumbling into the boat. Seals all around picking up fish. Then the unexpected, Grandfather always said to expect it and be ready for a shark. No shark this time though. A huge seal after the herrings, had trapped itself in the net and the net starting to rend. We would lose the fabled silver tube, and no one would believe us. Without thinking I picked up the gun and shot the harmless creature. There was blood in the water despoiling the silver tube and the dead weight of the seal was too much for Winston who got his foot entangled in the net and was dragged overboard. It was a disaster. I hauled and hauled. The nets tore apart and I was left with the broken end and a few fish. Winston was gone and all because of my greed or ambition to catch the silver tube. I felt at that moment that I should join Winston and drown myself, there and then. Who would carry the news of the disaster back to my dear wife? I broke down and cried for Winston and the poor seal and for my wife.*

*I sat in the boat for hours until the small buoy LT appeared to signal low tide. I could not land back on shore until the large buoy bobbed on the surface signifying high tide. For twelve hours I fought with my conscience and my foolishness. More than foolishness though, just over-ambition to be the first to catch the silver tube. I swore that I would serve a self-imposed penance for my actions in the hope that God would find a way to forgive me. A few days later Winston's hat and plimsoll were washed up on the beach, that sacred shore. All that was left of him until a week later his body turned up.*

*My wife died shortly afterwards of a broken heart. There was no one after me to pass on the stories. It was meant to be Winston. I had ruined everything.*

*I started collecting pebbles that were tossed up by the waves, to represent the silver tube of herrings that was lost and for the memory of Winston. I will return them to the sea and scatter his ashes where I lost him when the seven boxes are filled, and my penance ends.*

I returned Winston's photograph to his shrine, put the key back into its hiding place and burned Father's story. The painted pebbles I removed from the locker. They filled the final places in the seventh box by the white wall. I waited until late November and on the first high tide I took Grandfather's plumb line and all the boxes of pebbles to the place marked on the chart. The top buoy of the plumb line bobbed on the surface confirming high tide and the depth, seven fathoms. I tipped the pebbles back to where Father believed they belonged.

The next night I rowed out with the two urns. When I reached the buoy, I lay back in the boat imagining the herrings dancing in the cool depths, rubbing up against one another. The females shedding their eggs like stars first born into a Milky Way of fertility. I knew then that God forgave Father his fatal mistake and was ready to send his and Winston's soul to swim with the herrings. I scattered their ashes into the sea, together once more, and watched them drift into the depths to join the eggs of the herrings adhering to the pebbles returned to their rightful place.

I knew also that soon the eggs would hatch, releasing the young herrings to replenish the ocean. There they will gather in shoals and Winston will regale them with stories of his great-grandfather who sailed the Seven Seas.

*'It is an ancient Mariner and he stoppeth one of three...'*

But Father's story will never be told.